Ann Schweninger

Birthday Wishes

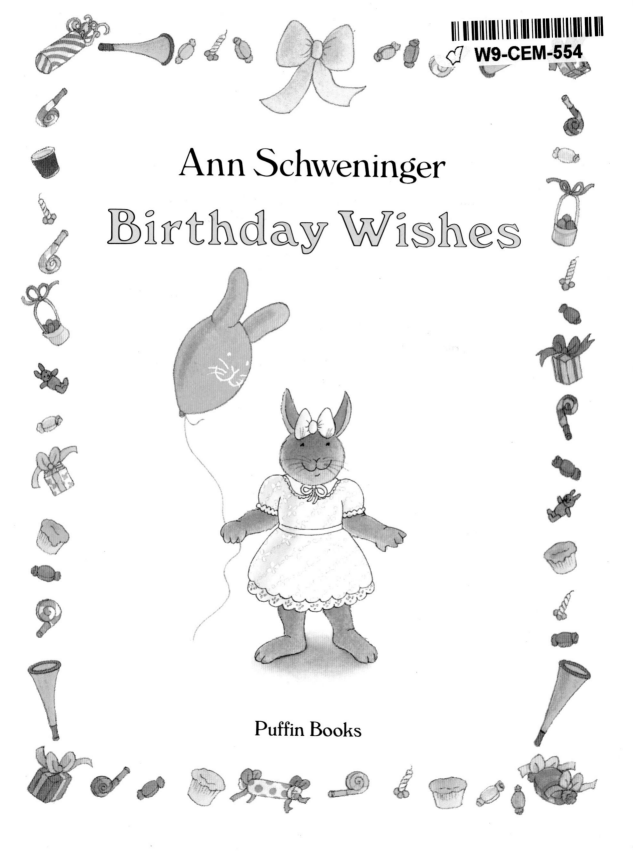

Puffin Books

For Geoffrey Hayes

PUFFIN BOOKS
Viking Penguin Inc., 40 West 23rd Street, New York, New York 10010, U.S.A.
Penguin Books Ltd, Harmondsworth, Middlesex, England
Penguin Books Australia Ltd, Ringwood, Victoria, Australia
Penguin Books Canada Limited,
2801 John Street, Markham, Ontario, Canada L3R 1B4
Penguin Books (N.Z.) Ltd,
182–190 Wairau Road, Auckland 10, New Zealand

First published by Viking Penguin Inc. 1986
Published in Picture Puffins 1987
Copyright © Ann Schweninger, 1986
All rights reserved
Printed in Japan by Dai Nippon Printing Company Ltd.
Set in Bookman Light

Library of Congress Cataloging in Publication Data
Schweninger, Ann.   Birthday wishes.
Reprint. Originally published: New York, N.Y.: Viking Kestrel, 1986.
Summary: The Rabbit family's festivities for Buttercup's fifth birthday
make all her wishes come true.
[1. Rabbits—Fiction. 2. Birthday—Fiction. 3. Parties—Fiction.
4. Cartoons and comics]   I. Title.   PZ7.S41263Bi 1987   [E]
86-25485   ISBN 0-14-050682-9

Getting Ready

Presents

I don't know what to give Buttercup for her birthday.

Let's look at Buttercup's list—

Birthday List

roller skates
paints
dresses
bicycle
bubble gum
piano
tea set
doll
umbrella
sandals
puzzle
make-up set
puppet
yoyo
bracelet
toy bear
kite

Buttercup's Birthday

Party!

Happy birthday
to you!

Happy birthday
to you!

Opening Presents